T0129822

Two Sisters

—— ESTER ELENA TIERNAN ——

iUniverse, Inc.
New York   Bloomington

Two Sisters

iUniverse books may be ordered through booksellers or by contacting:

iUniverse
1663 Liberty Drive
Bloomington, IN 47403
www.iuniverse.com
1-800-Authors (1-800-288-4677)

ISBN: 978-1-4401-9598-3 (pbk)
ISBN: 978-1-4401-9596-9 (cloth)
ISBN: 978-1-4401-9597-6 (ebook)

Printed in the United States of America

iUniverse rev. date: 12/3/09

<>< ><><> P R E F A C E <><><><>

Marion and Mayina lived in a small village nestled at the base of the mountains, leading a pleasant and easy life amidst the goodness and the humility of the people.

They did not imagine how events would twist their destiny, bringing them to a different stage in their lives. They would be confronting circumstances, secrets and events that coalesce to disturb the routine of their lives.

They will endure situations that will open the doors to hope, desire and love; testing their faith on the Supreme being, guiding them with their values, to forgive and comprehend those around them who have erred.

Strengthened by the knowledge they received from their parents about union, love, broadmindedness, respect, work and integrity, they will know how to bear the daily vicissitudes that will come their way.

<><> CHAPTER ONE <><>

When, many years ago, Vicente and Celestina Mangual arrived in this beautiful and tranquil place, the village became their and their daughters' promise of a bright and full future.

Don Vicente was a generous and gentle man, very affectionate with his wife Celestina, and his daughters Marion and Mayina.

Celestina was a woman who loved her husband and saw her daughters as a blessing from God. The two girls filled her whole life with their play, games and banter, which was all she needed to be a happy woman.

Their marriage was founded on mutual respect and revolved around the girl's daily activities. They where good parents, hard working, thrifty and cautious regarding life's choices, but generous and loving toward each other.

They taught them the simple life and this forged their characters; goodness and sacrifice for others. That was the legacy they left for them and it served as a guide in their lives after these two good and kind people died years before in a terrible accident.

These two girls were very special, their good qualities and behavior distinguished them from the other children in the local school. The long and curly hair, the big dark eyes and the angelic smiles, made the parents feel proud and happy with their lives.

When Celestina looked at them, she rejoiced with the sweetness these two angels, spread in her life. Although life was good and pleasant, there nevertheless was something in her that caused her grief, something from the past that she concealed and which lingered like a dark shadow in her mind. She knew some day, that pain would be exposed and that gives her anguish and makes her shudder.

<><> CHAPTER TWO <><>

Mayina was contemplating the rainfall against the window. It was dark and very cold. Sitting at the corner of the room, between the shadows created by the small lamp that illuminated the Hotel entrance; she watched how the water rushed without direction or course in a swirl of bubbles that drifted with the current …

In the solitude of the night, she was thinking, that her life was the same as at the rain pounding at the window. Although young, she felt the years where quickly passing by. Hoping and waiting that life would bring her someday, the happiness that always dreamt about.

She didn't know that, in the next few days, everything would change in her life.

Marion, her older sister, looked on her with sadness, toward the way she spent the time in fancy and absurd dreams. She thought that way because in her life, nothing was special or promising.

Her daily routine was her total dedication to the restaurant and the hotel.

She looked older than a 35 years old woman and was not as pretty as Mayina.

The daily work did help her keep her very attractive figure. It gave her the air and confidence of a strong woman, with a special beauty that was reflected on her smooth and fresh skin, like the petals of flowers.

<<<>>>

<><> CHAPTER THREE <><>

Outside, the rain and the wind pounded the place with furry. Absorbed in her dreams, Mayina did not notice the arrival of the last bus from the Big City and the passenger that descended and hurry up to the Hotel entrance.

Thinking that she was asleep, the passenger approached her and in a soft voice, spoke to her, at the same time that she woke up from her enchanted dreams. With a surprise gesture, she greeted de passenger and excused herself for her behavior.

His name was Mariano Avolea and was looking to rent a room for few days.

In the village he was informed that in the Hotel of the deceased Vicente Mangual, now under the administration of her daughters, he would find a good place to stay, clean, decent and very affordable.

She gazed at him and thought, "What is a man like him, so different, good looking, well dressed, refined, cordial, doing in our village?

The only visitors this village had, once in a while, where travelers passing by, toward and from the mountains.

In the recording book, he wrote that his address was in Wendarral, a town very close to the Grand City, near the coast and the principal Port and his profession was a former Lawyer from the Supreme Court.

<>< > CHAPTER FOUR <><>

Marion was finishing her work for the day, checking that everything was ready for the next day. Hearing voices outside, she entered the doorway of the dining room.

Since he was arriving so late at night, she assumed the traveler had made a long trip and hurried to greet him and offer him something to eat.

Once he had retired to his room, Marion looked at her sister and said, "I'd like to know what brings this man to our little village of Caceres. He has such a formal and well-bred look about him, but something about him…. The look in his eyes…makes me think…."

Mayina, who had not yet recovered from her amazement, let loose a laugh and answered, "Oh, so now you're able to see the future in people's eyes! I'd sooner stick with my incurable dreams! Goodnight, Marion"

And with that, she drew the front window curtains, closed the entryway door and before retiring, looked in the cash box at the day's revenues from the Hotel and Restaurant.

Walking toward her room, she was aware of the rain and wind pelting and blowing with furry. It brought to her mind "when rain falls with such force it cleans and remove impurities that are dragging to the riverbed". Why then, isn't the cycle of human life like that of nature, so that, all things are washed away by a good soaking?

With a big smile she entered her room, knowing that her imagination and comparisons were sometime funny and silly.

<<<>>>

As she was getting ready for bed, her thoughts turned to the recently arrived guest, and her curiosity led to reflect on the reason for his visit.

How long he will be staying, and many other questions as she let herself sink into the cloak of sleep, giving thanks for what life had giving her and smiling at what strange and curious things might yet happen to her.

She was awakened by, the crowing of Lorenzo, a rooster so old she no longer knew his age and who, everyday at the same time, practiced his crowing. The aroma of toast and brewing coffee snapped her out of her lethargy.

The morning promised a day of brilliant sunshine. When at last she left her bedroom, she went quickly to the dining room. There Marion had almost everything ready for breakfast and Teresa, their only employee, was setting the tables.

The Hotel belonging to the Mangual sisters was well known in the area for its delicious coffee, hot chocolates and breads and pastries fresh out of the oven each day.

<><> CHAPTER FIVE <><>

As she did every morning, Mayina started her day serving her waiting customers; their delicious hot coffee with milk, frothy steamed hot chocolate, accompanied by their famous anise pastries and little buns with crisp fried pork rinds; biscuits and muffins. Teresa baked them every morning with such care, to the delight of all those who tasted them. Those lucky ones were well prepared to face the long and cold day ahead.

The Hotel was a wonderful place to begin the day; there, everyone would congregate early in the morning to discuss events…. from the lighting of the local square, the expenditures of the mayor's office, the movie shown at the local movie theatre the night before to, how many piglets the police chief's sow had given birth to, or whether the Cortez' cow was eating fresh pasture or hay.

Everything was critiqued in the most cordial manner…somewhere between laughter and guffaws…but with the intention of presenting, defending and generally looking after the affairs of the village that they all value so much.

Mr. Avolea was also seated for breakfast, enjoying his coffee, reviewing papers that absorbed all his attention and distracted him from the conversation of the locals around him. In any case, those were their own affairs, nothing to do with him.

Mayina's curiosity drew her to his table; she offered more coffee, which he accepted with a friendly smile. She asked him, almost coquettishly, if he had had a good night, if he found his room agreeable, if he had been cold or if Lorenzo the rooster's morning call had wakened him.

To which he replied with a smile that everything had been fine, thank you…

Noticing that she discretely directed her gaze at his papers, he folded them and placed them in the briefcase that he had place in the chair next to him.

Realizing that her curiosity had been noticed and that, in any case, she couldn't learn anything further; she drew away toward other tables. Still, she could feel his eyes following her throughout the dining room, and it made her blush.

That morning, there where more customer than usual. The night bus had brought various tourists; a group of religious pilgrims, most of whom were nuns and elderly women on their way to the monastery in the mountains. Among them was a priest, noticeable amidst all the women for his years, which where few. There was also a group of hunters sitting and talking at a large table.

Mayina couldn't help thinking, when looking at the two disparate groups in the midst, that one represented life and creation, and the other represented death and destruction....

During the course of the morning, they heard that the nuns were on a spiritual retreat, accompanied by Father Tomas who, after the retreat, would be meeting with the local parson.

From the moment of his arrival, the young priest was delighted with the village. He had been raised and spent all his life in the city, and he couldn't get over the peacefulness of the village and the kindness of its folks.

One of the nuns told Mayina that he had been found at the door of the convent 27 years earlier and had been raised lovingly by the sisters as though he where their own son. They had molded him into a man with a good heart and a gentle soul.

Although it brought them great sadness, they knew it was time for him to leave their world and experience life beyond their world.

The newly arrived hunters were going to a shooting match in the mountains. The competition took place annually at this time of year; at the end of the match, winners would receive prizes and awards.

A the morning progressed, the dining room was emptied of its clientele; there was only the sound of dishes being washed and the low murmurs emanating from the kitchen where already preparations had begun for the midday meal.

<><> CHAPTER SIX <><>

They were nearly finished tidying up their work in the dining room for the midday meal when Mayina noticed, under the table and hidden from view by the tablecloth draped over them, some papers left behind by Mr. Avolea. She picked them up and, her curiosity piqued, tried to discern what was written on them, hoping to learn something more about the man. With disappointment, she discover that they were pages filled with numbers, revealing nothing of what she had hoped to learn, mentioning only something about the Forest Zone. Imagining that they were of importance to him, she left hastily to find and return them to him.

She found him in conversation with Don Javier, the town's taxi driver. As she approached she heard him ask about the location of the Forest Area. Don Javier unfolded a map of the area, placed it on the hood on the car and pointed to the spot on the map.

They were about to leave when he glimpsed Mayina running excitedly in their direction; handing him the papers saying, "I found these under the table where you breakfasted and I thought you might need them".

Mariano, taking the papers in his hand and smiling at her, replied, "Thank you very much. They have to do with a planned project, and I really appreciate your thoughtfulness."

As he was leaving, he looked at her intensely, in a very particular way that made her blush and which she interpreted as a compliment.

She watched, as the car grew distant, heading toward the mountains; remained in place until they were lost from sight, leaving her wrapped in sensations she had never had before but felling very happy.

Turning toward the Hotel, she sensed that someone was watching her; she turned around and saw no one, only some children running towards the town square, so she hurried along her path towards the Hotel.

<<<>>>

In the next few days, Mr. Avolea continue with his daily routine, breakfast and dinner, and the rest of the day spends in the Forest Area.

Although she pretended otherwise, Mayina was gnawed day and night by her curiosity, wondering why this man about whom no one knew anything had come from the city to this place. But he seemed to bring luck with him; there was more and more work every day at the Hotel, and Mayina had a notion that with the arrival of this man a new phase in their lives was beginning.

<>< > CHAPTER SEVEN <>< >

The change in temperature could already be felt…the cool mornings, the sky clear and limpid, and, with the warmth of the sun, the aromas of the flowering herbs flowed down from the mountains. Their fragrance spreading throughout the valley, offerings up its torrents of perfume and announcing the arrival of the season of flowers and fruits.

In the evenings, after all the routine hustle and bustle and when time permitted, the two sisters would meet to discuss the details of the business.

With the arrival of the milder season, they had to decide on a renovation to enlarge the dining room, the hiring of at least two more employees to give a hand to Teresa, updating of the décor in the bedrooms, and general expenditures.

Mayina trusted her sister unreservedly and these meetings actually bored her. What she desired was that her sister would find love someday, and so she not had to listen and make decisions about things she didn't understand.

Her frustration was palpable, and although they had dealt with this issue several times, nothing had every resulted from it. She saw Marion as a solitary person, living only for the business, losing herself in it and neglecting her own life.

It had come to the point that her personality had changed. She dressed plainly, whereas in reality an attractive and elegant woman. She needed someone to partner with her, pamper and love her.

For Mayina, life was a layering of bounty, a huge bouquet of flowers and she knew that someplace she would come upon someone destined for her, she would fall in love, and find her happiness. She sensed it, she dreamed it, and she imagined that this would all come to her some day.

But she saw that these feelings were lacking in her older sister.

When they were finished with their meeting, Mayina decide to go out and take a walk in the surrounding's of the house. It was a lovely afternoon. The shadows by the trees bordering the property danced in the to and fro of the breeze. At the thought of these trees, she remembered that they had been planted by her parents when they had first arrived her, and now, with every day they greeted their shadows and fragrance of the flowers, especially at this time of the day when they mingled with the sweet smell that poured down from the mountains and their own garden flowers, completing the enchantment of this special place....

Mayina closed her eyes and breathed the lovely air, filling herself with the freshness and incomparable sense of peace.

She sat down to contemplate the meadows and the plains around her, the mountains, and all the rest that represented all she knew, and that she understand was all hers and made her feel protected and happy.

She was sitting there, absorbed in her thoughts, when she heard footsteps coming in her direction.

Se realized it was Dario, Teresa's son, who had been born a few months before her.

"Hello, butterfly", he said. He had called her that since they had been childhood playmates.

He said that butterflies were soft and delicate, restless and frolicking. Although fragile, they possessed a great desire for life.

He saw her this way…full of life, pretty, sweet as a flower's nectar.

They loved each other like brother and sister, had been raised together and went to the same school, sharing their joys and disappointments. It was said that Dario felt a little more than, different from a brother's caring, but people didn't know what bond united them.

<<<>>>

<><> CHAPTER EIGHT <><>

Life was pleasant, full of hopes and dreams in which the image of their parents was the foundation of their lives, <Mayina thought>. They had pampered them, raised them in a circle of love, work, honesty and goodness. Very rarely did she recall that terrible day when her parents died. All that remained was the sorrow and loneliness of those awful moments.

The loss of these two beloved beings had left the daughters at the mercy of an uncertain life and without the safety and the guiding hand that they had provided.

There had been hard times for the two, but little by little they had pulled out of the lethargy that had overtaken them. With the help of Teresa and Dario, they continue the business for which their parents, has sacrificed so much.

Despite herself, her sister Marion, being the eldest, assumed the responsibility of continuing offering room and board and Teresa, the loyal employee, sheltered and protected them with her caring in those difficult times. In time they managed to transform the small guesthouse into what it was today, a lovely hotel.

Dario was a good son, respectful, hardworking and honest. For many years he had also helped with the hotel and becoming familiar with all aspects of the business. The sisters embraced him with complete confidence, entrusting him with any and every aspect of its activities.

The coming of the new season brought new tourists and many people in search of work, many hoping to leave the distant city. There were no vacancies in the hotel; the dining room was always filled to brimming morning and night, and a reservation list guarantee that there would be a full load of work in the coming three months.

Mayina was always adept at instigating conversation with the tourists. Many of them told her that in the Forest Zone a very large enterprise was flourishing, ranging from mining to agriculture. They were looking to hire help, people who where willing to put down roots in the area. This gave the place an air of excitement.

At the daily breakfast, one heard continually of how important the area had become and the opportunities and advantages that would accrue to the town's residents as a result of this enormous project.

No one knew who had been the initiator of the enterprise. It was generally believed to be some foreign company or some wealthy Arabs or someone who had won the lottery and thereby been able to finance their business dreams. In the end they were all mere guesses that did not lead a path to the benefactor and which no one was able to ascertain.

Mayina thought that Mariano Avolea had something to do with all this; he, however, was not particularly forthcoming on the subject. He decided that she would find a way to ask him about it.

All day this thought churned around in her mind. When, finally, she had a free moment, she commented to Marion about it. After hearing her out, Marion told her "that as long as he follows the rules of the hotel and pays on time---which he did—there was not and issue. She also asked her, that regardless of her curiosity on the subject, to please refrain from commenting, that if Mr. Avolea were indeed behind these changes, sooner or later they would know about it, and in the meantime they should focus on their work, which, after all, was quite a lot these days."

Mayina didn't like to be scolded by her sister; it hurts her feelings. She didn't understand her curiosity and her desire to know things.

"You're still very young in this business; <Marion added> we need to be deaf to what others say around us. Mr. Avolea comes from Wendarral, where people are good and quiet and keep to themselves. When I was there for my studies, I got to know a lot of folks in the city, good families, refined and wealthy."

Her sister was a person of few words. 1n fact, she almost never spoke of anything unless it had to do with the business.

For this reason, she was surprised and delighted to hear her, talk like this.

She would have liked to hear more on the subject, but Marion, with a gesture of dismissal, replied, "It's getting late; I'll tell you more another time."

<><> CHAPTER NINE <><>

They were just finishing arranging the dining room for lunch when Father Tomas arrived.

They hadn't seen him for several days, and he greeted them excitedly. "I've just been informed that I now belong to the Child's Chapel; my transfer has gone thru and it fill's me with great pleasure".

It was his first appointment as a priest, and it means that he would not longer be near the nuns that he loved so much. However, he felt an irrepressible happiness to know that he would be living in this village, which he called Eden because of its charm and beauty.

Marion and Mayina received the news with much rejoicing, knowing what it meant for the young priest. Exchanging hugs, they invited him to celebrate his happy news by serving him a bowl of the broth, reserved for special occasions.

He was young and full of life, with a desire to do good works, whereas by now Father Jacobo, the eldest of all the priests, could no longer conduct mass or does much of anything in the chapel. With the passing of the years, his eyes and his memory had both faded, and lately he spends much of his time praying or visiting the sick.

He had been the village's first priest, arriving many years ago in Caceres, "with the goal of savings its residents from their sins", as he would often say. It was he who drew his words from the Supreme Being, who had build the church with the help of the entire village population. The church proved both their faith and their pride, as it was both simple and welcoming.

Some time afterward, Father Stanislaus arrived to help him as Parish Priest, accompanied always by his sense of humor and his hearty appetite.

He had been born in Greece, which had lent him a mystical quality, bringing with his priesthood different customs from the locals, but was accepted by them.

But what bound them to him were his generosity, his rectitude, the love he professed, his simplicity and his palate. For him, the simplest of meals was an exquisite delicacy. For all of these and the human warmth that he radiated, made him a very special person.

<<<>>>

With so many new tourist and other visitors, Teresa and Dario remarked on the need for more help at the hotel. It became impossible to finish a day's work, and with that in mind, Marion decided that it was time to hire more help as they had discussed before.

This fell to Sara and Carmela, who, under Dario's guidance, took care of the rooms and the laundry, freeing up Teresa to continue creating her daily delicacies for the guest's delight.

The two new employees also worked as needed in the restaurant. They were good women who came highly recommended, although Carmela need a bit of guidance; she was something of a chatterbox, taking interest in everything going on around her. Sometimes this expressed itself thoughtlessly as disdain and ill will toward current gossip, which was running aplenty of late.

<<<>>>

<><> CHAPTER TEN <><>

The morning dawned cloudy with lots of rain and wind. The rain pounded with monsoon strength, flooding the valley, paths and all the lowlands at the foot of the mountains.

During breakfast Mr. Avolea remarked to Marion that, as his stay was prolonged beyond his original expectations, he would be beginning to look to purchase a house and car.

Returning for dinner, he wanted to make inquiries with them about these plans, but as Don Javier, the taxi driver, was in a hurry to drive him to the Forest Zone, as was their daily habit, he finished his meal and left in a rush.

Although the weather forecast had provided for the rain to stop in the afternoon, the sky appeared overcast and no clearing was in sight. In any case, in the restaurant lunch and dinner were prepared as usual.

Amidst the thunder and the bolts of lightning, Fathers Stanislaus and Tomas arrived, shaking their cassocks as they entered by the door on the patio. As they grumbled about the storm that God had sent them, they approached the counter, remarking that some of the parishioners who had been sheltered at the church told them that, when passing through the zone of the Sleeping Hills, they had seen Don Javier's car stuck on the side of the road. They were unable to approach, since the river had overflowed and obstructed their path.

Dario, hearing what had happened, offered to go and give them a hand since they were stuck in an area where the river flow was quite intense and flooding could be very dangerous. He would try to reach them on horseback. Some guests offered to go along with him on their mounts, and others volunteered to go along in their truck to carry any rescue material that might be necessary.

They were all getting ready to go when Officer Nicolas Puerta and the Police Chief Federico Caruso also arrived and immediately offered to join in. They carried what was needed in the truck and left, but not without accepting a stiff drink to carry them through the storm and the cold.

Mayina, unaware of what was happening, stood watching the rainfall, a habit she's had since childhood. In her innocence, she found everything magical and fascinating. To her it was a though threads of silver fell from the sky, sprinkling the ground with its sweet nectar, overflowing its edges like chocolate on a giant cake.

She remained there for a long while in front of the window until Marion came in and shattered her trance.

When she told her what had happened, Mayina looked at her with fear and agitation.

Marion hugged her, saying, "Don't worry, everything will turn out all right. It's probably something wrong with the car, you'll see. In a few hours they'll be back", she reassured her, caressing her little angelic face, and then withdrew toward the kitchen.

Her heart was filled with worry at the thought of Mr. Avolea and Don Javier broken down in the midst of the storm with no shelter from potential flooding.

She didn't like having unpleasant thoughts, but some intuition told her that they were in peril. In the last few days, she had been having premonitions that, with the arrival of so many strangers to the town, they were being watched, indeed observed, and this troubled her. She remembered seeing amongst them one group wearing hats and wide sunglasses and carrying thick bags like those used for mountain climbing. What caught her attention was that it was not yet very sunny and really not cold enough to warrant such clothing, leading her to imagine that they didn't want to be recognized or they sought to hide something.

She would have wanted to remark upon this to Marion and Dario, but thought it would be better to wait to reveal her thoughts.

<><> CHAPTER ELEVEN <><>

The policeman Marcelo Aronca had stayed on the police station to see how the situation progressed. The town's population had grown in the last few months, but it still maintained its regular quiet rhythms.

When words began to circulated, some townspeople approached the church to make inquires, but Father Stanislaus, not really knowing first-hand what had happened, was unable to tell them much, and asked them only to pray for them and the rescue party.

The task would not be easy, the waters were churning and the current was carrying stones in its path with great force, putting at risk anyone who might fall into the rising waters.

At the hotel a few people clustered, hoping to help or learn some news.

The hours passed slowly and although the rain had finally stopped, the winds were still very strong and storm clouds were moving away heading towards the south.

Daylight was fading; giving way at dusk to a rainbow with magnified the beauty of the sky on the plain, looking as though it were floating to the rhythm of the fierce current. Worry was palpable amongst those gathered there awaiting news, making the wait seen even longer.

The group on horseback headed cautiously toward the area where the car was reported to have being seen. Flooding had reached the point of the highest fields. The view was spectacular; it was as though an enormous lake had formed, covering the entire area; only the tip of a few trees stood their ground with stoic valor, against the current.

The truck advanced slowly and with difficulty, as the road had in some parts disappeared, making the trip all the more dangerous.

Finally, after few hours, the rescue party was able to reach the spot known as Slipping Hills where they could see that the car, protected by cliffs, was safe from the current. The rain has stopped, and only a few clouds skittered by toward the horizon; the river roared as it rushed out of control toward the valley.

Dario headed up the group as they approached the vehicle; he called out to Don Javier and Mariano, but there was no answer. He saw that the windshield had shattered into a thousand pieces. As he drew nearer he realized with horror that both men were injured and bleeding badly. He opened one of the doors and, touching the men, confirmed that

they were still alive. Swiftly and capably, the men wrapped their bodies with blankets to protect them from the wind, which was still blowing hard.

They prayed that they would have time to get them to the clinic. To that end, they slid the injured men in the back of the truck, where bedding had already been prepared. It was clear that their wounds had been caused by firearms and not by an accident caused by the storm.

They made the return trip to the village by a different road, one that skirted the hills, a road with two advantages; it was both faster and safer.

When the truck left, the Chief Caruso and Officer Puerta stayed to further investigate the circumstances of the incident.

There was no doubt about it; they had been shot. The windshield and door revealed bullet holes from a long-range rifle. They wondered what the motive could be, since the intent had clearly been to kill, but the rain and wind had caused the murderer/s to falter some error of judgment.

Don Javier had taken shots in his shoulders and legs, the attorney, in the head, arms and ribs.

Once police had wrapped up their investigation of the site, they joined the rest of the group who were fording the river on horseback.

They arrived near twilight at the village and went directly to Dr, Acuna's Clinic to report the incident to him.

The town had no hospital and Dr. Acuna was the only doctor in the area. He oversaw childbirths, broken bones and much more; for more serious cases, people had to cross the mountains to the hospital in the Grand City.

Acuna immediately had his staff prepare for the arrival of the two wounded men, the doctor alerted the hospital, asking them to urgently send an ambulance, doctor and specialist in case they proved necessary.

When the truck arrived with the patients, a group of people had already congregated at the clinic entrance, wanting to know what had happened and how serious the injuries were. They were shocked that Don Javier who had served them so many years with his taxi was now the innocent victim of a violent attack.

<><> CHAPTER TWELVE <><>

The rescue had taken several hours. When Dario arrived back at the hotel, he was tired and soaked from head to toe. He felt as though the cold wind had penetrated to his bones, and knew that he needed to change clothes and drink something hot.

Marion and Mayina worried and waited anxiously for him. As soon as they saw him and learned details of the attack, they rushed to the clinic, which was located a few blocks from the hotel.

They entered via the emergency room entrance; there they met the Police Chief who told them that Don Javier has suffered only lacerations and that he was expected to make al full recovery. As for the attorney, he had several gunshots wounds, one of which was in the head and quite deep.

The doctor entered and approached them; they worriedly inquired asked after Mariano, since they already knew that Don Javier was out of danger. "His condition is very delicate; he has lost a lot of blood and his vital signs are very low and weak", he said.

"It wouldn't be wiser for the moment to transfer him to the hospital, as he has bullet wounds that reach quite close to vital organs, which makes it more dangerous to move him", he continue. He had administered first aid and was now resting with sedation to prevent any movement that could provoke further loss of blood.

All this disturbed Mayina, who couldn't manage to understand what had happened.

Sitting in an armchair in the waiting room, her heart went out to Don Javier and especially to Mariano who had no friends or family to attend to him.

She shuddered to think of the worst that could happen, but what se really didn't understand was why this event was affecting her so much and in this way….

The Police Chief approached them and suggested that they return to the house, "For the moment, no one can do anything more and, whatever happens, we will notify you immediately.."

Mayina offered to spend the nights at Mariano's bedside, but the Chief, thanking her for her offer, said, "Father Stanislaus and I will keep vigil here in case the doctor needs us.

Father Tomas, along with Marion and Mayina, proceeded out towards the church to pray for the speedy recovery of the two injured men. When the church service was over and they were waking towards the hotel, Mayina commented to Marion about the group of people they had seen and why they had caught her attention, and her reasons for thinking this way.

Marion, as Mayina had expected, began her usual never-ending sermon to which she was by now accustomed, and even her sister didn't believe her and got annoyed, she would talk with one of the priests or with the Police Chief. Her intuition told her that the group had something to do with the attack that just happened in the hills

<><> CHAPTER THIRTEEN <><>

With evening came a warm breeze and stars, which shone in their entire splendor. It was dinnertime, and as the sisters reached the hotel, they found Dario very busily attending to the customers who that night filled the dining room completely.

In the anteroom of the restaurant, several guests were patiently waiting to be seated; it appeared that the events of the day had whetted their appetites. Sara and Carmela were in the kitchen helping with the preparation of the meals, which under Teresa's supervision, and to the delight of all diners, each dish took on a magical quality. As they taste her savory creations and discussed the particulars of the day's events, they were all surprised that something like that could happen there. There had of late, with the arrival of so many visitors to the village, been a sense of uncertainty and insecurity in the village.

A it was nearly midnight when the last of the diners left the dining room and the staff was putting the last touches on preparations for the following day, the sisters closed the dining room for the night.

Meanwhile, as Marion was reviewing the receipts, she commented to Dario what Mayina had confided to her. He also had notice the same group of people, but as so many guests were arriving each day, both for the hunting tournament taking place in the mountains and the festival in the town, he hadn't given much thought to it.

He suggested that they should be more cautious and attentive to the comings and goings of the hotel's guests. The business was vulnerable to such people; moreover he noticed that tonight's diners were quite worried about the day's events.

That night, sleep did not come to Mayina; the day's tragedy kept her awake. Rising from bed and putting on her robe, she went into the kitchen to make a cup of tea to calm her nerves and assuage her anxiety.

All around her silence; all she could hear was the tick-tock of the big clock in the dining room. With her cup of tea in hand, se sat down at one of the tables, breathing in the soothing aroma rising from the warm liquid. As she sipped, it filled her it the warm sensation she had hopes for.

In the solitude of the dining room, her thoughts turned to Mariano and what could possible have been the motives for the attack on him.

In truth, she knew almost nothing about his life or his past, He was gracious, likeable, respectful; she like his way of talking, even the way he walked and dressed. Without being able to put her finger on it, a strange sensation had taken possession of her, accelerating her heartbeat. She had an enormous desire to be with him. She thought next of Don Javier, an innocent victim of his tragedy. He was a good man and known by many as such. He had for many years lived on the outskirts of the village with his wife Dorita and his children Agustin and Luciano.

Immersed in her thoughts, she didn't notice that dawn was breaking, bringing with it the brightness of a new day, pouring in through the large windows of the dining room.

Tired, sleepy and lethargic from lack of sleep, she returned to her bedroom.

When she later went downstairs for breakfast, she found that she hadn't been the only one to pass a sleepless night. Those already seated at the tables had haggard looks of having spent a watchful night and replaced the lost energies with a succulent breakfast.

In contrast to other days, that morning everyone was quiet and somber, embedded in their own thoughts; the dining room was engulfed in an unusual silence. Fathers Stanislaus and Tomas, emaciated and with dark circles under their eyes, began their day very early. They already had offered the first mass and had visited the clinic, and now found relief with fried eggs and ham, coffee and milk and hearty toasted bread.

They brought the news that Don Javier was recovering well and felt a little better but that Mariano, who had undergone surgery well into the dawn, was in critical condition. One had to hope and let God decide.

<<<>>>

<><> CHAPTER FOURTEEN <><>

As the hours passed, Don Javier responded positively to his treatment. If he continued apace, he would be discharged from the hospital in a few days. His wife Dorita who had spend the night at his bedside in the clinic was showing signs of fatigue and worry. When she received the report of his progress, she returned home to share the good news with her sons.

When Chief Caruso was notified of Don Javier's improvement, he went to visit him and to ask him a few questions. As he recounted what he could remember, the poor man shook with panic, remembering how the shots penetrated the metal of the car, his terror of dying in that lonely place, and how he had been paralyzed by fear even though he wasn't aware of having been wounded.

Seeing how upset this made him, the Chief thought it better to wait a few more hours before taking the man's statement.

He eliminated the idea that the accident had been caused by the storm; the case was now officially classified as a suspected homicide.

The investigation grew more complicated; without knowing the motives or holding any suspects, he would have to inform his superiors of the accident, which he was not looking forward to. He knew that the townspeople were unaccustomed to the methods usually employed in such investigations, but he had no choice in the matter.

For the moment, Mariano, could' not explain what had happened because by his delicate condition. He would wait a few hours to do so. In the meantime he assigned Officer Puerta to remain on guard at the clinic, keeping an eye on patients and visitors alike, and keeping them well away from the area where the injured and sick were treated. They suspected that whoever had committed the attack might strike again if they learned that the men were still alive.

In the statement he made that morning, the Police Chief advised caution to the locals and others who were aware of the investigation. He wanted to be absolutely certain not to miss or lose any lead in the case; he also requested that whatever they had seen or remembered about the last few days, be immediately reported to the police.

At the hotel, news of a different nature began to arrive, creating tension amongst the tourists. Despite the newly arrived lovely and gentle weather, no one had any desire to ride horseback on the plains or take walks in the meadows. Although no one would admit it, they were afraid, and it showed on their faces. Some took strolls in areas deemed safer; others remained close by, cautious, hoping to learn further details about the attack.

The Police Chief awaited the arrival of one of Mariano's relatives from the Grand City; He also wanted to revisit the hotel room where perhaps he would discover something suggesting a motive for the attack.

However, he had to wait for authorization or the arrival of a family member to allow him entry to the room.

After various attempts, they were finally able to make contact with Mariano's sister, who, as soon as she learned of the attack, immediately left the city for Caceres.

During their conversation, she said she had no idea what would have provoked such an attempt on her brother's life. "Mariano appears to have no enemies. During his career in the courtroom, he conducted himself with honor and professionalism; he had a large circle of friends that certainly included no one who would have wanted to take his life."

With each passing hour, the Chief's concern grew; nothing would lead one to suspect that the motive was revenge or some sort of betrayal. In his mind until now the case seemed to be leading to one of mistaken identity. However, he still had to wait for the investigation to conclude.

Late that night, a woman arrived at the hotel. She was young, but her face bore traces of fatigue and fear. She arrived in the company of Father Stanislaus and Chief Caruso.

She gave her name as Monica Avolea, sister of the wounded attorney. They had first stopped in at the clinic to see Mariano, but due to the lateness of the hour, they decided instead to have a late meal at the hotel.

After they finished their dinner feeling the effects of her long day, Monica said goodnight to the others and withdrew to her room. The Father left a few minutes later.

Before leaving the dining room, the Police Chief asked if guests had anything new for them or if anyone had any fresh memories to report regarding the case. Mayina, who had been listening with great interest, commented on what she had observed a few days before, expressing her worries and emphasizing that this group of persons, congregated in the village center and that she had seen them when she returned home from the clinic and again after Mass.

He listened attentively and asked her details while writing notes in a small notebook; anything might eventually be useful towards the resolution of the case. Before finishing his coffee, he remarked, "tomorrow will be a very difficult day, however, I as well as all of you… need the rest".

Meanwhile Dario closed up the business and reminded the sisters that, what with all that had happened and all the comings and goings of so many guests, they had failed to clean the room that would eventually connect to the new dining room, which was now in construction. The workmen had already prepared everything to connect the two rooms; they had only to do so as soon as possible.

Mayina offered to do this last chore, despite being full of sadness. Everything in this room, had been left to them, by their parents; and since their deaths, no one had dared to touch anything in it. Nevertheless, she would have to begin the following day.

<><> CHAPTER FIFTEEN <><>

With the intention of accomplishing her promised task, after breakfast, Mayina began her chores. She asked for Dario's help in moving the heavier items and for the truck to carry away the discharged items.

With some trepidation, she opened the door of the room; the smell of so many years of enclosure rushed out at her and made her shiver. Somewhere in between the penumbra and the darkness she seemed to see ghost-like silhouettes dancing before her eyes.

Overflowing the room were pieces of furniture, books, toys from their childhood and thousands of other things. Choking back tears, she lit a small ceiling lamp and began the task. Staring with the most accessible, she formed small piles so that Dario could easily load up the truck.

With each item she touched, she felt as though the past would recover from its long lethargy---photos from childhood, of her parents, of her sister, from schoolwork including a few pieces of handiwork made from a woolen fabric that her mother had carefully stored. In each box or bag, the past bubbled up to the surface, carrying her back to times almost forgotten. There was so much to do and to decide upon.

She continued fastidiously to do the sorting; building more and more piles until, amongst the things that she had sorted through, and she found a small music box which se did not remember ever having seen before.

She found it amongst some very pretty curtains that her mother had told her came from Europe, brought by her grandmother on her honeymoon.

As though she had discovered a hidden treasure, she sat down and gingerly opened the box. As she lifted, she heard the last notes of the Blue Danube, her mother's favorite waltz. She also found some coins and old paper currency as well, along with a few photos of her maternal grandparents and her mother when she was little.

At the bottom of the little box was an envelope with handwriting damaged by the years; she opened it with great care. Inside was a document and another sheet of papers. As she unfolded the document she understood that it was a girl's birth certificate, with a birth date identical to that of Marion, but with a different family name.

A few moments passed during which Mayina tried to deny what she was looking at. She drew closer to the small light to read what the card said, and who had written it; it expressed great thanks to Celestina and Vicente, her parents, for accepting to take Marion into their home. She had been born a few days before in Wendarral; her parents had not been married. As she, the mother was very young and under pressure from her father, she felt obligated to act contrary to her emotions, and to make the terrible decision of giving the baby up for adoption.

Admonishing them to love and care for her as though she were their own, she herself promised never to interfere in her life.

Mayina remained stunned for a few moments and could barely believe what she had just read. Everything seemed confused, unbelievable and extraordinary.

"So, Marion is not my sister?"

Her eyes began to brim over with tears, obscuring her vision and making it difficult to continue reading.

"But who, then, were her parents?"

As much as she could, she continued reading.

She read: Mother, Valeria Pineda. Father, Juan Manuel Avolea.

"Avolea?

A relative of Mariano Avolea? "

Leaning back, she cried in anguish; not because the love she felt toward her sister would be different, but because her parents had kept the secret and did not confide in them, did not tell them the truth.

Her parents always treat them equally. "What reason did they have to keep this secret?"

"Did Marion have knowledge of this secret?"

If not, "How she will let her know?

What anguish, what uneasiness and distress. Once again life was sweeping her up into something she could never have expected. My Lord, so many questions without answers!!

<<<>>>

<>&<> CHAPTER SIXTEEN <>&<>

She remained, for a long while, numb and submerged in her thoughts; she wasn't aware that Dario was watching her from the stairway, surprised and perplexed at Mayina's behavior.

Silently, she handed him the paper so that he, now, would share this unexpected secret with her.

A few minutes passed and, seeing that she continued to cry, he drew near and embraced her, calming her with these words, "Mayina, my beloved little butterfly, this changes nothing; everything will continue as it was. You have to understand that a piece of paper isn't worth and has no bearing on everything you've experienced during a lifetime with your sister. She's your sister, and nothing…absolutely nothing… should change between her and you.

They remained like that, saying nothing, for a long time. In their minds thoughts of the present and past dance unbridled to the rhythm of their heartbeats.

Eventually, they recovered their calm; to Mayina was restored the serenity necessary to finish the task of clearing out the room.

She kept the papers in the music box, wrapped it up with the curtains and silently left.

As she passed the dining room and saw them, Marion asked, with a look of concern.

"Have you found some hidden treasure amid all the mementos?"

Upon noticing her parent's favorite curtains, she lifted them with great delicacy, as though to touch them was to caress their much-love faces.

As she placed them down, she did not realize that within the folded fabric lay her hidden past.

Marion wasn't aware of what the other two were feeling at that moment, as they answered evasively, "Nothing important, only these curtains…they're the only things that are really usable; everything else is old and worn and has been damaged over time."

"What a shame," answered Marion, "but I'm happy to know that they can be put to good use again."

With the stress evident in her expression, Mayina mentioned to her sister how much she had been affected by seeing all the items that brought back memories of her parents.

She told her she wished to go and pray for them, and to soothe her own spirit.

Knowing how vulnerable Mayina could be, she agreed that she should go to church, but on condition that Dario go along with her.

When arriving at the church, they went directly to Father Stanislaus office. He was concluding a confession with a parishioner.

When he saw them, he embraced them with his well-known kindness; he sensed that something very important had led them to the house of God. "My children", he inquired, "How can I be of service to you? I am here for your every need".

With tears in her eyes, Mayina handed the old piece of paper to the priest who, with humility in his heart, began to read it.

When he finished perusing the papers, he sat down next to them, embraced them again and said, "Mayina…lovely example of your parents…They opened their hearts and their home to a small human being who came into this world by an uncertain path; this being is your sister who knows nothing of her origins. She is innocent of her circumstances, as were you. Let us leave today's events in the hands of God. He will know when and how Marion will know the truth. Do not be disturbed by this information. Pray; ask God for the strength to maintain the secret for which He, in his infinite wisdom, will illuminate the path to fallow."

<<<>>>

<>< CHAPTER SEVENTEEN ><>

Marion was concerned that her sister, upon coming from church, enclosed herself in her room. She understood that sorting through and removing the contents of the unused room had affected Mayina strongly, and that she was suffering the effects of her emotions.

"Right now that lunch is beginning and I most need her help....", she thought.

"When I have a few free moments, I'll go to speak with her."

Lying in her bed, Mayina spent her time recalling her childhood, her parents, their lives, everything. What she learned today, she could scarcely believe. To discover something like that after so many years...

She was unable to comprehend how something of this magnitude might impact them both.

Her head was swirling with questions, some without forthcoming answers that left her feeling even more despairing.

"Why were her parents, she wondered, silent about the circumstances of Marion's birth?"

All these thoughts led her to the realization that, in fact, she know very little about her parents, only that they had been important to her and her sister. What mattered and gave her comfort was the love and affection that she felt for her older sister. It didn't really matter that they weren't blood relatives; they were sisters of the soul.

When she prayed she asked for God's help to guide her through these difficult moments when she so needed support.

Her worst fear was that her sister when learning these facts would abandon her or estrange herself.

A few gentle knocks on the door brought her back to reality. It was Teresa, come to keep her company for a few minutes, as she always did, whenever Mayina stayed in her room at length.

She confided in Teresa and loved her with all her heart; it had been Teresa who had filled the empty space left by her parent's deaths. She would have liked to confide in her now, to tell her what she had discovered, but this was different. Recalling the priest's words, she simply muttered, "Teresa, I have such a bad headache."

Teresa covered her with a blanket, closed the curtains and gently kissed her forehead. Before leaving, she turned and looked at her sweetly, saying, "Rest, my dear, it will do you good for both your body and your mind."

Mayina felt that Teresa had read her thoughts

<><> CHAPTER EIGHTEEN <><>

Mariano was recuperating slowly, responding to the treatment and care he was receiving at the clinic. Dr. Acuna informed Chief Caruso as his condition improved. The chief, waiting in the hallway, entered the room but, seeing the state he was still in, thought it imprudent to force him to speak. He made it known, however, that he insisted on making a statement.

He began, saying, "The only memory I have is that we were driving in very windy and rainy weather when suddenly we heard an enormous noise. Then the windshield shattered, so we crouched down to take cover, thinking that a stone had hit the car. But then we heard more, and on contact with the metal, they exploded like bombs, so we knew that they were gunshots. Don Javier, panicked, asked if I was OK; he yelled that he was crouching down and that the shots were aimed at us. When the shooting stopped a few seconds latter, I carefully moved towards the back of the front seat and saw that Don Javier was bleeding profusely and crying in pain. In a state of shock from the explosions I wasn't aware that I was also wounded. When I saw that the danger had passed, I took off my overcoat and covered Don Javier with it. After that, I remembered nothing else."

The chief remarked that when they were found, Mariano had fallen on the back of the rear seat, unconscious, like Don Javier.

He had wanted to continue with his questions but Mariano seemed very tired and sleepy, so he let him knows that his sister Monica had arrived last night in Caceres.

Dario, who had kept busy in the grounds of the hotel, could not calm his mind, thinking of the events of the day. As he tried to busy himself, Carmela appeared, saying that he was needed inside. As he approached the hotel, a very attractive woman was getting out of her car. He admired her for a few moments, without noticing that she also was observing him. It was the first time in her life that she had experienced such a sensation.

She introduce herself, she said her name was Monica, Mariano Avolea's sister.

Dario, who had not yet emerged from his state of enchantment, reached for her suitcases, managed to mutter his own name and hurriedly entered the hotel.

Marion was watching from the entryway and notice that Dario was blushing and seemed flustered.

Smiling, she greet the guest who continued to look, with special interest, at Dario…

<><> CHAPTER NINETEEN <><>

When Monica entered the restaurant for breakfast, Chief Caruso was already enjoying his second coup of coffee. When he saw her, he invited her to take a chair at his table.

Mayina, approached to greet her, carrying a plate of morning pastries which Teresa had just finished baking. As she poured her coffee, she asked about Mariano's condition.

Monica answered that she had just returned from seeing him, and that he seemed to be making progress. Looking at Mayina and Dario (who were watching from the counter), she thanked them warmly for all they had done for her brother.

When they where ready to leave, Monica moved towards the counter to ask Dario if, in his free time he would be willing to take her around the area and see the scene of the accident. Without ceasing to look at her, he replied that he would be delighted and that he'd be happy to take her wherever she wanted.

When they had walked off, Mayina went up to him, place a hand on his shoulder and said, "Dario, dear boy, in case you didn't notice, Cupid has struck you with his arrow."

Without answering, he hurriedly left the dining room.

Marion, who had overheard, chided her, saying, "Those are issues of the heart and one doesn't joke about such things."

<<<>>>

As the days passed, the place returned to its normal rhythm, letting daily necessities resume their usual prominence.

The hotel and the dining room with its noisy clientele once again became the preferred meeting place.

Dario and Monica went out every day on horseback to explore the surrounding area; Mariano progressed in his recuperation and Don Javier can be seen with his wife Dorita, strolling though the streets of the town.

Security forces provided people with the stability and peacefulness to continue their daily routines and they had detained the group reported to the authorities and they were transferred to Caceres for the investigation.

Mayina however, continued her solitary ways, engulfed in her thoughts. She came to know that Juan Manuel Avolea was Mariano and Monica's father and that he would be

coming in a few days to visit his son. Monica was gladdened that she will see him soon and he will see how well her brother was, and he will discover the town and its surroundings with which she had falling in love, both for is natural beauty and that of its people.

Mayina, upon hearing the news, came apart, to such a point that she could not eat nor do her customary work in the hotel. She roamed from one place to another, as though lost in her own world. The employees had heard her crying in her room during the day. Carmela disclosed to Marion what they had overheard.

She imagined what was the cause of Mayina's upset, and she vowed to speak with her that night.

<>< > CHAPTER TWENTY <><>

Dario and Monica had been riding along the river since the early morning. The landscape was spectacular, the rushing of the water as it ran along the rocks served as soundtrack to the tranquility of the place; the trees rocked to the beat of a gentle and cadenced breeze, inviting them to dismount.

Leaving the horses free to enjoy resting in the shade, they sat down on some large boulders at the foot of a willow on the edge of the river.

Gazing at the sun's rays dancing in the stream, Monica broke the silence, asking Dario, "Have you ever been in love?" These words caused a strange warmth to come over his face; he dropped his face and, ashamed of his shyness, answered yes.

Looking at him questioningly, and wanting to know more, she asked, "Tell me, who is the lucky woman that holds your heart?"

He couldn't contain the words that gushed forth. "Since I first saw her, I couldn't stop thinking about her. When I saw her for the first time, my heart began to beat desperately and I've felt that, with every day. Something is missing in my life, like the air I breathe, in order to stay alive. You know, I've never felt anything like it before, for any other woman."

Hearing him speak with such love about his feelings, she said, "I hope your love will be returned and that you'll be very happy with her."

She got up quickly and, standing before Dario's dumb-founded look, she jolts her trousers and began walking back to where the horses were resting.

"Wait! Now you! You haven't told me if you had ever been in love."

Reproachfully, she turned around and, looking at him almost with anger, replied,   "Yes, very much, but the idiot didn't even notice."

Seeing her reaction, Dario, got up and drew her near, took hold of her hands and looked at her. "He's not stupid, only afraid of being rebuffed or not being loved in return."

Feeling the warmth of his hands, Monica whispered, "Dario, tell me please who holds your love."

Delicately he kisses with intensity and his caresses with love and passion. They remained in this embrace for a long time, he stroking her blond hair with the sun shining in it like gold threads, she clutching his body, so strong and tender that it made her tremble with pleasure.

They gazed at each other and kissed, both of them feeling the first sweet buds of love…

<><> CHAPTER TWENTY-ONE <><>

It was growing dark, when they started the return trip towards the town, feeling that their hearts were beating in unison, a great love…

Marion was on her way to her sister's room where she had retreated a while earlier.

Gently knocking a few times, she opened the door. She walked in and sat on the edge of her bed, and, very gently, stroke her hands. She saw in her a young woman, pretty, sweet and angelic, a sister she loved. She didn't want to see her suffer; she wanted to do something to prevent her unhappiness. But she wasn't given a chance; her sister elude her, withdrawing nervous, sad and absent. She would give so much to see her happy again. With her beautiful and wild dreams, her spontaneous and roaming thoughts, her song-like laughter that she so missed of late these days and which gave her so much joy.

She pondered her sister's situation, trying to read her mind, to know what grieved her so.

Poor thing, she thought, all these recent events have affected her profoundly. Dario is the only person who can pull her out of this despair, although with Monica's arrival, they hardly see each other anymore; he's always busy taking her to discover the surroundings or to ride horseback in the hills.

Could this be what is disturbing, Mayina so greatly, and causing her to act so strangely?

Could it be that Dario means something more to her than was thought?

I don't think so, but the, Lord, what ails her? If I could read your mind, if you would confide in me, I would so love to help you, my sweet sister."

Mayina kept sleeping, so Marion kissed her forehead and very slowly left her room.

She felt drained, beaten, exhausted, as though the weight of all these years had suddenly landed on her shoulders. She felt alone, very alone, and the tears began to spill down her cheeks.

On her way to her room, she heard voices coming from the vestibule. It was Dario and Monica, the two embraced, kissing each other like children, playing at love.

When she arrived in her room, she dropped down on her bed and began to cry out all her sadness. She felt her failure as a woman, without the care and tenderness of a man to protect her, to be with her, to love her.

Everyone believed that she had everything in her life, when in fact she had nothing of what a woman longs for.

She cried and laughed; in her head everything was upside down. She was on the verge of despair, even though no one would know this from appearance. But day-by-day she was feeling worse.

A long time passed as she remained plunged in her sadness. Then she stubbornly shook it off and promised to change; she had lived alone by her parent's wishes, neglecting her sister and postponed her own possibilities for womanly happiness. What matter now was Mayina; she needed Marion now more than ever and she had to be strong for her, but she had reached the point in her life to make a decision.

She cried until she had no more tears, until disheartened, begging God not to abandon her, she collapsed into the tranquility of sleep.

<<<>>>

<><> CHAPTER TWENTY-TWO <><>

In the morning, Teresa approached Marion, hugged her and said, "You're looking tired and drained, you should think about taking a few days off. It's been years since you did. You work hard all day, and it will do you good.

Smiling back at her she replied, "Soon, very soon, I will, but for now there are other problems that need to resolved." And with that she resumed preparing the dining room for breakfast.

She understood that her life had to change; the daily routine that she had been living prevented her from finding happiness. Her experiences of the previous night brought to her understanding the enormous solitude in which she found herself. She had to open the doors to her heart in order to allow room for the love that she so needed and longed for.

Linked to her own troubles was her sister's unhappiness. She couldn't imagine what so weighed upon her. She remembered that her behavior had changed since the day she and Dario had tidied the old unused room. What could she have seen or found that so changed her state of mind, she wondered.

Not knowing filled her with anguish, leaving all else by the wayside. It wasn't only sifting through all those things from the past that grieved Mayina; there was something else, something both sadder and more profound that had upset her, and she intended to find out what that was.

<<<>>>

Dario and Monica had left early to go to the church and speak with Father Stanislaus.

They went to receive communion as a couple, which they did with great pleasure. From there, they went on to the restaurant; they were excited and happy to share their happy decision with everyone there. They went hand in hand into the place; approaching Teresa and the others, they kissed gently to show how in love they were. The diners all applauded, wishing them much happiness in response to such happy news.

Teresa cried with joy to see that her son had met an ideal mate; Marion remained speechless and only managed to embrace them both; Mayina, her eyes filled with tears, wished them good fortune.

Everyone was happy and moved. Then arrived both Fathers Tomas and Stanislaus and some friends; as they entered they greeted the couple.

Next arrived Mariano, accompanied by a nurse, surprising everyone gathered there and adding an extra layer of pleasure to the couple's delight. Mariano wanted to celebrate with them this happy occasion.

Mayina, still somewhat amazed by everything, gave Mariano a hug, and taking his hand, let him toward the group.

They took their seats at the large table in the dining room and took their breakfast together, like a big family.

During this little celebration, Mayina seemed to consider Mariano in a new light, as though she had discovered something very special in him. At the same time, Mariano responded with smiles and small gestures that did not go unnoticed by anyone in their company.

To celebrate the new couple's announcement and Mariano's recovery, it was decided that they would hold a religious service at the end of the week.

<<<>>>

<>‹› CHAPTER TWENTY-THREE ‹›<>

Chief Caruso was to hold a press conference at the city hall to make public the findings of the state security forces, which had been working on the case in conjunction with those from Caruso's own department.

They had apprehended the suspects of the alleged crime; the criminals had confessed their involvement in the offense.

For this reason, Caruso wanted to inform the public about the details of the investigation, before the suspects were transferred to the city for trial. A the same time, he was awaiting the arrival of Juan Manuel Avolea, accompanied by his attorney Alejandro Zamora who had taken on the case on behalf of the authorities.

As he was preparing for the press conference, he received an urgent message. Upon reading it, his face lost all color. Something completely unexpected concerning the case had emerged, and his silence was requested until the facts could be corroborated.

In the hotel, in hopes of enhancing Mariano's rest and recuperation, a large room was being prepared for him, a room with large windows, which had been salvaged from the former bedrooms.

From this room, he could see the mountains in their entire splendor and the meadows where the magnificent river meanders amidst the willows and aspen, showcasing the real beauty of the spot.

Mayina was in almost daily contact with Father Stanislaus, confiding her troubles and her worries. She panicked at the thought of handing over the old papers to Marion and also the thought of Juan Manuel Avolea's arrival in the village.

The priest, with his typical patience and understanding, listened with infinite love as she unburned her troubles to him. He understood her fears, which had completely overwhelmed her. Making her feel insecure and alienated. She wanted, as much as possible, to stop tormenting herself, and she hoped that when Juan Manuel Avolea arrived…with God's help…all would be resolved.

She left the church with a lighter heart and great hope that happiness would some day return to her life. Mariano's arrival that morning had filled her with pleasure; although he needed some care, he appeared alert and I good spirits.

<<<>>>

She helped him settle in to his new room with its magnificent view of the valley, and he was grateful for his new practical and beautiful surroundings.

<She was feeling something new and different, never before experienced, and it was   visible in her face, the desire to be with him, and to helping him>

When she was about to leave his room, he said, "Later on, I would love to take a walk in the garden if you could manage it"… without even letting him finish his sentence, she answered, "I'd love to!…. I'll come in time to take a walk before diner…."

<>< > CHAPTER TWENTY-FOUR <><>

The hustle and bustle of the morning had left him tired out. The nurse helped him to lie down and rest. In the silence and solitude of the room, his thoughts went to Mayina, her gentle gaze and good-humored frankness.

He slept soundly; drunk with the perfume of the flowers that had graced his room. When he awoke, he found her sitting next to the large window, and he was moved at the idea that she had held watch over his dreams, like a guardian angel.

Once ready, arm in arm and walking slowly, they moved towards the garden. The sun shone brightly; it was very hot and somewhat humid. A breeze blew down form the mountains, tempering the blistering heat.

They walked through the gardens, which, at this hour, were shaded by the pretty grove of trees surrounding the grounds.

Mayina chatted animatedly, recounting the history of the village, telling of when her parents had arrived here, and of her childhood years, and when her parents had died.

He listened with interest, all the while admiring her attachment to all the things that had made up her life.

Along the bank of the path, they came upon a bench placed at the foot of a luxuriant tree. As he sat down, Mariano broke off a flower and place it her hair. He spoke of how happy he was to be in this place of tranquility and goodly people, so different from the city.

He also, spoke of his childhood, of his solitary life, of his profession.

During a pause, Mayina, feeling the need to know more about him, asked, "What were your reasons for coming to Caceres?"

He answered, looking at her, "Exhaustion, physical and mental, and the desire to do something meaningful, to live differently. One day when I was young, I heard my father say to a friend that someone very special from his youth lived in the area of Caceres. I imagined that it had been an affair, or an impossible love that he remembered with tenderness. When I finally made the decision to make a change in my life, since I couldn't think of any place, I decide to begin here. From the moment I arrived here, I tried to learn something about what my father had said, but I was unable to learn anything."

Mayina would have liked to tell him what she knew, but recalling the priest's words, she preferred to keep mum about it.

<><> CHAPTER TWENTY-FIVE <><>

The conversation was interrupted by the arrival of the nurse to remind him that it was time to take his medicine.

Once back at his room, Mariano kissed her gently on the cheek and whispered that he had enjoyed the walk immensely, and most especially, her company.

Returning to the dining room, Mayina experienced a sensation of flying rather than walking.

Seeing Marion, she ran towards her, gave her a big hug and kiss and said, "I love you so much, big sister!" Marion, surprised by such a sweet outburst, cried tears of happiness.

Dario and Monica's relationship was only a few weeks in progress when, so sure were they of their feelings, they decided to marry.

To this end, Monica decided to travel back to the city to attend to all the plans and preparations. She invited the two sisters to accompany her; this way they could rest a few days and help her select her trousseau.

Marion was delighted to accept, on the condition that it will be only a few days, as she also wanted to be present at the public statement by Chief Caruso. As for Mayina, she preferred to remain and help Teresa and Dario with the hotel and restaurant.

They decided to leave after the religious service the following Sunday. They would travel by car so as to retain the most flexibility in getting around, but also to be able to enjoy the magnificent scenery provided by the mountains and the valley at this time of year.

Eager to take a short vacation, Marion was careful to make sure that everyone knew how things were to be done in her absence. She trusted them but wanted to be sure that everything would continue as per usual.

That Sunday the church was overflowing with attendees. In order to please all those present, Father Stanislaus and Tomas celebrated a join mass.

Mayina, Marion and Teresa sat in one of the last pews whereas Dario, Monica, Mariano and Clara, the nurse, sat in one of the first rows.

The emotion present in every spoken words and each song was palpable during the service. The sermon was beautiful, full of love and gratitude towards God, giving thanks for Don Javier and Mariano's recovery, as well as blessing the new couple with eternal happiness.

<><> CHAPTER TWENTY-SIX <><>

When the service was over, the couple and the rest of the group, gathered at the church door to greet the parishioners.

Mariano looked at Mayina and found her to be as beautiful as an angel. He moved towards her greeted her and kissed her cheek, letting her know how beautiful se was.

They walked arm in arm towards the restaurant. The morning was full of sunlight and enticed them to stroll through the quiet village streets. On Sundays shops opened for business at noon, giving stragglers a chance to enjoy their well-earned rest.

Chatting and enjoying each other's company, they arrived at the restaurant where Sara and Carmela, who had prepared a nice table for the entire group, awaited them.

Marion, who sat down next to them remarked, "Mariano appears to be completely returned to normal." "It's entirely due to the care given me by my guardian angel," he answered, gazing at Mayina.

As the event was winding down, Marion approached her sister to say goodbye. She hugged her and said, "Ill miss you a lot. You are the loveliest thing in my life; take care of yourself. You can't imagine how happy I am to see you so fulfilled."

Monica and Marion were ready for their trip. They loaded their suitcases in the car, said goodbye to everyone and took off for the city.

The road meandered amidst the mountains, displaying the incomparable beauty of the valley as it stretched out towards the infinity. At every turn in the road one could see the village evaporating in the mist of the distance.

As they traveled they spoke of their lives, their dreams and their memories. They kept each other so entertained that they weren't even aware of the first city buildings as they appeared on the horizon.

They were traveling on the main highway and, as they reached a square, Monica turned onto a side road leading to a nice little neighborhood dotted with tile-roofed houses with gardens and grassy yards. When they arrived at number 508, Marion parked the car between two garages. A narrow border led to the main entrance.

As they opened the large door, two handsome dogs ran towards them. Hearing voices, a good-looking man came out and hugged her, at the same time telling her how much he'd missed her.

When he saw Marion, he greeted her, looking at her with certain surprised expression.

Monica embraced him and, turning to Marion, said, "This is my father Juan Manuel Avolea."

<><> CHAPTER TWENTY-SEVEN <><>

Smiling, she greeted him with an outstretched hand and had a vague sensation that made her shiver.

Juan Manuel noticed her movements with unusual attention; when he spoke with her he looked at her as if to find something that had once beguiled him.

Excited to be back at home, Monica gave him the latest updates on Mariano. Once they were seated in the large room decorated comfortably and tastefully, Monica explained to her father the reason for her return.

Surprised and moved by what his daughter had just told him, he hugged her and told her how happy he was for her.

Leaning back in an attractive armchair, he said, "Tell me everything that's happened, but beforehand, tell me where you managed to find such a lovely friend."

Monica was surprised and said, "But papa, didn't you get my postcards? In them I wrote all about where I was staying and who I was with."

"No, my daughter, I didn't get any mail and I was worried about not getting news from you, but---knowing how you are---I knew that sooner or later, you'd be in touch."

"You knew that I was in Caceres because of Mariano's accident; it was there that I met Marion and her sister Mayina who own the village hotel. They gave me all the moral and spiritual support that I needed from the moment I arrived."

In them I found the sisters I always wanted but never had, papa, and it was here that I met Dario my fiancé and future husband."

As he listened to his daughter speak, Juan Manuel's face became a grimace of anguish, fear, surprise and uneasiness.

Attempting to maintain his composure, he looked at Marion and asked, "What were your parent's names?"

"Vicente and Celestina Mangual", she replied, without really understanding what was happening and the reason for such a question.

To Juan Manuel it seemed that the earth was opening under his feet; his mind was roiling like a whirlwind. He couldn't be certain, it had all happened a long time ago and was buried in memories of his youth…" Why now, why would she appear after so many years? "He asked himself silently, as, in his mind reappeared faces which he used to know and which he believed by now were almost forgotten…

<><> CHAPTER TWENTY-EIGHT <><>

Expressing concern for the delay of the refreshments, he withdrew from the room, Monica notice Marion's confusion about her father's behavior, and commented, "He hasn't been the same since mama died, and he's not the same as he was. Also, Mariano's situation has kept him quite worried. I hope I'll be able to bring him some happiness with my marriage. Come", she said, taking Marion's hand, "I'll show you your room and you can rest a bit".

In the afternoon, after they rested from their long trip and unpacked their bags, they decided to go out and explore the city.

I was very hot, so Monica folded down the roof of her car so as to better enjoy the breeze and admire the dimming of the day.

They went around the outskirts of the city, admiring the surroundings. When they reach the city center they decided to park the car and walk.

They had gone a few blocks when Marion noticed in a window display of bridal gowns a beautiful dress. Monica wanted to see the dress up close, so they went into the shop.

A salesclerk who was busy arranging clothes on hangers asked if they needed any help.

When Monica said she wanted to try the dress in the window, she called the shop owner who had created the marvelous gown.

From a distance they watched a very elegant woman of medium height as she gingerly handled the dress.

As the approached they saw a slender woman of natural beauty that the years had not faded. They were surprised to see that her facial lines, eyes and her lovely smile were like those of Marion.

Noticing these similarities, Monica commented, "They say that we all have, somewhere in the world, someone who could pass for our double, and yours, Marion, is right here."

The woman looked at them stony-faced, silent, paralyzed and hearing Marion's name, collapsed in a faint.

<<<>>>

<><> CHAPTER TWENTY-NINE <><>

Summer had begun in the valley, all leafed out and with the scent of the fields in bloom. The air by now had lost its chill, and combed over the plains with the undulating rhythm of a magical dance. Each day's wakening, with the bird's songs and trills, invited all to savor the beauty of the natural world.

The village was in flower in muted seasonal colors, opening its imaginary doors and welcoming the happy visitors who swarmed to its delightful enticements.

In the hotel, as in the dining room, the tourist season was in full swing.

Dario occupied with his responsibilities, was missing his new love, counting the hours before her return. Mayina, who had once been separated from her sister also looked forward to her return.

Since she had been accompanying Mariano on his daily walks, he had begun to feel happy and restored.

Their conversations were pleasant and interesting. The more she listened to him, the more she felt his honesty, loyalty and generosity, and the more she felt the desire to share her secret with him.

The dilemma tortured her---whether it would do well or harm. She didn't want to wound her sister whom she loved with all her heart.

Why did it have to be her to discover the secret? To how many innocents would it bring harm if she revealed it?

When she confessed her fears to Dario, he recommended leaving it in God's hands; someday soon all this will right itself. " Dear butterfly, enjoy every day, think of what you have, what surrounds you, what is in your heart----that's what matters! Not what's written on a piece of paper! Don't feel guilty for having discovered something from the past; you're a victim of life, which is seeking its revenge. Bit by bit, all the tangled traps will finally meet their fate."

<<<>>>

<>∙<> CHAPTER THIRTY <>∙<>

Morning in the city invited recreation. The sky was blue with a few passing clouds that appeared like messages of mist that the wind blew in.

"Lovely morning, special to read and relax," said Marion, leaving the terrace where she'd been.

She went into the library where there were hundred of them. She was concentrated on reading the many titles and therefore didn't notice Juan Manuel seated in a high-backed armchair.

"Oh, good morning", she said, surprised by his presence. "I came to look for something to read. What do you recommend?

Rising from his seat, he moved towards the glass doors that protected his collection. As he showed her how to open them, he answered, "Here you'll find many that you might like".

He looked amongst them for something that might please her; he found one on the history of the city. Handing it to her, he remarked,

"I hope you like this one, it's very interesting. Also, Marion, I want to apologize for my behavior yesterday. You know, when I saw you, I was reminded of a woman I knew when I was young, someone that I loved very much and was never able to forget."

At that moment, Monica entered the room, looking for Marion to go shopping with her.

She would have liked to decline her invitation and continue to listen to Juan Manuel, but she decided to ask him to continue his story after dinner.   As for the book, she would read it another time.

She greeted her father with a loud kiss and gently pushed Marion, who was laughing at her playfulness, out of the room. As they walked toward the door, they came face to face with Alejandro Zucareno who had come to consult with him on some legal affairs. The attorney paused when he saw the women, effusively greeting Monica, whom he had not seen for several months.

Looking at Marion, he said, "Wow! And this lovely young friend, who is she?"

"Marion Mangual", she responded. She didn't like how he spoke to her. She shot him a look of disdain and turned around, muttering about his audacity.

Monica reached for her, laughing at his behavior. "You know", she said to Marion, "he's very vain. You gave it to him where he's most vulnerable, his ego. You handled him the right way and he deserves it. For him all women are the same. Poor fool, he doesn't' know who you are, Marion! "

Satisfied at having given a lesson to the indefatigable Romeo, they went down to the car and headed to the city.

<><> CHAPTER THIRTY-ONE <><>

They were both curious about how the shopkeeper and seamstress had recovered from her dismay and they wanted to have another look at the bridal dress that had so dazzled Monica, so they drove directly to the shop where they had been the day before, when the shop had closed, with the arrival of the ambulance, to give assistance to the shop-owner.

An employee greeted them at the entrance of the shop; when they asked after the owner, she answered, "Valeria is resting at home now; for several years, she had suffered from a bad heart, so any strong emotion can cause her upset."

Marion felt guilty for what had happened and expressed the desire to send her flowers. She asked the woman's name and address. "It will do her a lot of good, Mrs. Pineda loves flowers, specially lilies and jasmine".

"They are also my favorites." Marion managed to answer.

Monica had moved away towards the dressing room and now appeared in the bridal gown, dazzling with exceptional beauty. The bride's dress was magnificent; it made her look angelic. Marion burst into tears of joy, when she saw her; she realized how inspiring was being in love! Drying her eyes, she thought, "Some day that will be me in a beautiful bridal gown."

When the dress and all the accessories were wrapped up and ready to take to Caceres, the shop-owner suddenly appeared. She had requested to be contacted immediately, if the two young women returned to the store.

Emaciated and almost trembling, she drew near the women and with a very gentle voice told them that she would like them to came back and see her.

Looking at Marion like only a mother can look at her daughter, she said, "Many years ago, I lost my only daughter. Seeing you is like seeing her. I apologize for yesterday and I hope you can understand."

Turning to Monica, she then said, "It is my duty as creator and designer of the gown to be present at the wedding, to dress and help the bride. Therefore, Ms. Avolea, with your permission, on your wedding day, I will travel to the place where you will be celebrating you marriage."

<><> CHAPTER THIRTY-TWO <><>

Valeria Pineda, to see and hear her name, recognized her daughter. He heart told her!

This daughter that she had given, under pressure from her family and against all her best instincts and whom she remembered day after day, year after year, hoping and praying that God would give her the chance to see once more.

The moment had come and weighed upon her heart, already so weak from so much loss, and se was not willing to loose her again.

Her father and siblings had decided her fate, as was customary in those days, obliging Vicente and Celestina to move and raised her far away.

They banished the love of her life, Juan Manuel, ordering him never to seek her out again. They had her married to cover her dishonor, something to which she gave no importance. Her heart and all her being beat with her daughter.

The only things that remained of her were her first little baby clothes, which she would often hold and embrace with the desperation of her absence.

Life eventually grew less trying; death carried her husband away, leaving her alone with her memories and finally granting her this long-awaited independence.

So she then gave herself over to designing and sewing bridal gowns, pouring all her love and passion into each one.

She tortured herself over the weakness she had shown in the face of her family who had pressed such terrible choices upon her, over not having fought for her daughter, for her lover, for all that was hers.

God had heard her pleas! Finally the moment so long awaited had arrived, to see her daughter and her lost love....

<><> CHAPTER THIRTY-THREE <><>

Mariano had a final visit with Dr. Acuna who, satisfied with his patient's progress, declared, "Perfect! Now you can return to work, but only for a few hours at a time. Take things slowly, and don't overdo things. Follow my advice and in few days you'll feel completely back to normal." Before he left, Mariano thanked him for all the care he had given him.

Mayina was waiting in the clinic's hallway. As she approached him, she asked, "Is everything all right?" "Excellent", he answered.

They walked to the car that he had purchased a few days before; he opened her door and she got in. "I saw a house for sale that I'm interested in. Will you come with me to see it?"

"But of course. We women possess more gifts in this department than men," she answered, laughing at her own boldness.

"Good," he replied, "Well then, we'll see just how much wisdom there is in all that."

They took the road towards the Forest Zone where the undulating road, at the base of the mountains, towards the river. The immense view surrounding them was enchanting. In the distance they could see houses, granaries and farms dotting the valley like little spikes of flowers bursting forth from the fertile soil. Mariano commented, how much loved this place, how his life had changed and how happy he was.

He took a small road leading to an enormous hill in the esplanade where lay the home he was looking for. As they got out of the car, a man came out of the house and walked towards them. The property was small and in very good condition with an imposing view of the valley and its mountains.

The picture enchanted Mariano before his eyes. Taking Mayina's arm and looking at her sweetly, he joked, "So what were you saying about women and good taste?"

Mayina also captivated by the place, took in the picture silently. It was as though all his had been suspended above the huge valley

"Do you like it?" he asked. "It's precious, it's sublime, and it's spectacular! I congratulate you, Mariano, for your superb taste. This place will bring you the peacefulness and happiness you seek," she answered with sadness....

<<<>>>

<>><> CHAPTER THIRTY-FOUR <>><>

When they returned from their shopping, they ran into Juan Manuel on the patio who was waiting for them with refreshments. Monica, excited by the marvels she had purchased, hugged her father commenting, "Oh pappy, I'm so happy! Thank you for being so good to me. You know, the designer of my wedding dress is going to Caceres to help me. Poor thing, she suffers from heart trouble. When she saw Marion, she became ill and said she reminded her of a daughter she has lost years ago. What we notice most was that she has many traits in common with Marion."

Hearing this, his thoughts returned to his youth. Could it be possible that it was Valeria, he wondered?

His daughter continued speaking and he asked, "So tell me, who is this lady who made such an impression on you and that you have so much to say about?"

"Her name is Valeria Pineda and she has a boutique selling wedding gowns on Main St."

With his whole being, he shook with the realization that he would have to confess as soon is possible the whole story to his daughter.

When the two women went inside, he decided to go pay a visit to the boutique. He had to speak with Valeria immediately. On his way, his anguish turned into anxiety, just to know that she was alive. Years ago he had been told that she had died; for a long time he had silently cried over not to having been able to ask her forgiveness.

Once at the display window of the shop, he was able to see her inside, and he felt his whole being twist out of worry and desperation. He pushed the door and entered. When she saw him, she cried out his name and ran toward him.

They embraced and, weeping, repeated one another's name, wanting to gather up all the years of absence. Still embracing, they moved to the office of the shop and closed the door in the astonished faces of the customers and employees.

That evening Monica and Marion ate alone in the large dining room. Her father had called, letting her know that some personal affair would require his attention through until the following day; but that they should wait for him in the morning because he had something important to tell them.

<><> CHAPTER THIRTY-FIVE <><>

They were serving breakfast in the restaurant when Father Tomas arrived with the news that Father Jacob had worsened during the night. Dr Acuna had told him that given his age as well as his illness, it was only a matter of time before he would be called by Divine Providence.

Everyone heard the news with great sadness. The Father had shown great goodness and generosity towards all the people of the village. Everyone who was able to went to the church to pray for his soul.

At noon, he died. Many of the congregation gathered in the chapel to offer condolences and to help in the preparations for the wake.

They hung large black ribbons at the chapel's entrance, asking that all pay their respects to the priest who had given so much to the village and its residents.

Father Stanislaus and Tomas were feeling the loss of their mentor but nevertheless prepared for the religious service, which they hoped, would take place with the utmost respect and humility.

The chapel was decorated in a simple but elegant manner, with only candelabras and a crucifix where his body would lie for two days.

In the hotel the sadness at his death was palpable, even though everything carried on as usual for the guests.

Mayina appeared normal, however her apparent tranquility masked her grief over Father Jacobo's death. She had adored him, and now regretted that she hadn't been able to thank him for all that he had done for her.

More than ever she now missed her sister who had not been informed of Father Jacobo's passing. She expected her to return on Sunday in time to attend the funeral.

Meanwhile, Dario had his hands full maintaining the business and keeping thing running smoothly while Marion was away.

Mariano spend a few hours each day in the Forest Zone and doing the paperwork necessary for the purchase of the house on the hill.

This gave Mayina some dreaded feelings. Her life changed so much since his arrival, discovering each day new facts about love. When he moved away she would be draped in a cloak of desolation, for feelings that she had but couldn't not be fulfilled.

<><> CHAPTER THIRTY-SIX <><>

While waiting for her father to return that morning, Monica suggested to Marion that they take their breakfast on the terrace. The large house, with its many flowers and climbing vines, was bursting with colors. Wisteria and jasmine covered the pergola where butterflies and hummingbirds flitted from flower to flower. The garden was full of color and life. Marion was admiring her surroundings, "What a beautiful spot! It fills me with peace and tranquility."

"Thank you," answered Monica, "Mamma used to spend hours here, sitting and admiring the flowers; it reminds me of her. You know, she never spoke much, and nothing made her happy. Papa tried to give her everything; there was something about her that no one could ever understand. Often I heard her speak of someone, and it make her cry."

"How sad," remarked Marion, "that she had such a sad life. Everything here is so different from our town."

At that, the maid came in carrying a telegram from Mariano, alerting them to Father Jacobo's death. When she heard the news, Marion began to cry. Attempting to console her, Monica asked, "Do you want to go back earlier? The funeral is scheduled for Sunday morning."

"I would be grateful for that," she answered, drying her tears. "In any case, we've accomplished everything we needed to do for your wedding."

"We can leave tomorrow morning; that way we'll arrive at dusk," added Monica. "We better begin packing now."

As they made their way inside the large house Juan Manuel and Valeria appeared at the entrance. The two women looked at each other with surprise to see the two of them together, and, no less, holding hands.

"Good morning," they both said. The two women like statues, were frozen in their tracks unable to stop their amazement of the moment.

It was Juan Manuel who broke the silence. Looking directly at Monica, he said, "My child, when we are young we commit errors, we sin, we overindulge, thinking that life has a beginning and ends. But as years pass we are surprised to understand that all our mistakes are interrelated in such a way that only destiny has the ability to reveal."

'Papa, I don't understand what you're trying to tell me."

"Monica, I made a lot of mistakes when I was young, out of immaturity, fear, and cowardice. For me Valeria meant love. When I was very young I lost her because I didn't know how to defend what she represented in my life. Today, thanks to you and destiny, I've found her again. Do you realize, my girl?"

"No, really, Papa, I don't. So what was Mama in your life?"

"Your mother was a very good woman, she suffered from errors made in her youth as well, errors that I tried to lessen and which I will be able to make clear."

<>< CHAPTER THIRTY-SEVEN <><>

"Papa, I'm so happy that you met Valeria and that you also have the chance to be happy. I always felt that Mama wasn't happy. Who knows her reasons but she never confided in me. What she kept in her hart she took with her when she died. She tried to be a good mother and I love her a lot for that. I can't and won't judge you. Besides, you've been a wonderful father to me."

During this time Marion was listening to the conversation without understanding anything. Thinking that she had no part in it, she left them alone.

Monica, almost as a reproach, added, "You could have waited for another time to confess all this, Papa. When you arrived, we were getting ready to go back to Caceres tomorrow. I jus received a telegram from Mariano about Fathers Jacob's passing."

"I 'm so sorry, I was so happy and eager to tell you that I didn't realize. Beside, Marion has a part in this story."

"Look, Monica, I don't know if I'm doing the right thing in telling you all this; God knows I don't want to do harm to anyone, but Valeria has suffered all her life from my cowardice."

"Papa, what are you talking about? What has Marion got to do with any of this?"

"I will try to be understanding with you; out of our union a child was born, a daughter that Valeria loved very much. But her father and brothers, according to the strict rules of the times, forced her to give her up for adoption. The terms of the arrangement were that Vicente and Celestina move far away from them. They then immediately forced Valeria to marry a man that she didn't know. I, on the other hand, was told that she had died, so when I met your mother, I asked her to marry me."

Monica, stunned by her father's confession, could manage only to cover her mouth, to keep herself from screaming.

Her father took her by the shoulders and said, "My dear, you have to understand how many years of suffering we have endured; now we need to find some peace of mind. I'm sorry, when the two of you arrived together, seeing Marion and learning her name, I knew right away that she was my daughter. Marion Mangual is your sister!"

"Your mother and I paid dearly for our mistakes, we both brought guilt with us into the marriage. I only hope that you can understand and accept it."

She was only able to say, "Marion is my sister? My sister. Confused, she turned around and, in silence, went into the house to find her.

<><> CHAPTER THIRTY-EIGHT <><>

That night, Dario decided to close the restaurant early. The wake was in progress, and everyone wanted to attend. The following day, after the mass, Father Jacob would be buried in the local cemetery.

Mariano went to the concierge's desk and asked Sara where Mayina could be found. For the last few days he had seen her almost not at all. He wanted to invite her to attend the service with him and to share with her the pleasure of being the new owner of the house on the hill.

Sara showed him where she was; he found her with Dario. He greeted them both and gave her a hug, and mentioned how much he had missed her. She finished putting her accounts in order, and they went out to walk towards the garden.

"Is something wrong?" asked Mariano, addressing her silence, "It almost seems as though you're avoiding me. It's been days since we've spoken, and I miss you so much when I don't see you."

"I've been very busy. Anyway, it's better this way. I want to get used to it when you move to your own house," she managed to say.

She looked as though she were about to cry. With some effort she said, "I've grown used to your presence, to our afternoon walks. A few months ago, my life changed so completely; now loneliness will once again became my companion."

Taking her by the arm, he said, "What were you thinking, that you wouldn't see me again? I plan to continue to visit you if you want."

"I don't know, Mariano. I'm very confused; and I'm afraid. Besides, lots of things have happened; I feel overwhelmed and don't know how to resolve these things."

"Why don't you confide in me? Or haven't I earned your trust? Come. Let's sit down here and you can tell me," he said.

"I would like to tell you to relieve some of my anxiety so that you can help me. Even Father Stanislaus and Dario tell me to leave everything in God's hands and that I shouldn't worry. But I can't take it anymore, Mariano. These last weeks have been a torture to me. I accidentally discover a secret that my parents never revealed and now my dilemma is to make it known or remain silent."

"Mayina, it must be something very difficult for you to agonize over like this. If you decide to share it, I promise to help you and respect your secrets."

He then kissed her check very tenderly and, taking her hands, they walked together to the church.

Night descended on the area with its warm and welcoming cloak. Its crickets and lightning bugs began their nocturnal songs and dance. From the bell tower came the call to the faithful to pray.

<><> CHAPTER THIRTY-NINE <><>

While in the town Mayina and Mariano were trying to find their emotional paths, in the city Monica, Juan Manuel and Valeria were discovering their own new paths, paths that life and destiny had been braiding together for years.

This evening during dinner, silence reigned over the dining room of the large house. Marion, who didn't know what had happened that afternoon on the terrace, broke the silence by remarking, "It must be very lovely to meet again after so many years and continue with the same love. To think that it was us who led you to your destiny and helped make it happen."

"No, Marion, not us," Monica replied. "It was you!"

Juan Manuel, interrupting, added, "Sweetheart, it doesn't matter who it was, the important thing is that it happened, and this fills us with happiness."

Not wanting to be the one to tell the rest of the story, Monica said with annoyance and bitterness, "Go on, Papa, why don't you finish telling us the rest of the story."

"I don't think it's the right moment", he answered, looking at Valeria who, hearing the request, grew pale and started to tremble.

"Yes, please, begged Marion. Tomorrow we're going back to Caceres and I'd love to know the rest of the story."

"It's the saddest part of the story, and I don't think Valeria wants to tell", he answered.

Bringing forth as much strength as she could muster, she replied, "Life gives and takes many precious things. Finally it gave me the chance that I've waited for so long, to take back something that I lost and for which I have suffered and cried so much." She got up and went to the living room to get her handbag.

Marion didn't understand the meaning of her words. She looked at Juan Manuel and asked, "Did I do the wrong thing by asking and wanting to know?"

"I don't believe so, Marion, It's just that once we know the end of the story, it will cause you unhappiness, disillusionment and bitterness."

"I don't understand, why to me?"

Valeria returned with a small package and placed it on the table. She looked at Marion. With tears in her eyes, she said, "These belonged to my baby, the daughter I lost. The daughter that my father and brothers took, from me as a newborn and gave to people I didn't know so that the dishonor of the family would be forgotten."

She took out the envelope and handed it to Marion. "Take it, my little one. I kept this letter with all my love for all these years."

Distressed and afraid, she began to read. She covered her face and began to sob.

<><> CHAPTER FORTY <><>

Dawn was breaking in the city. The night's fog was giving away to the first rays of sunlight. A few stars defied the powerful sun and continue to twinkle in the vastness of the universe.

Juan Manuel and Valeria were still in the dining room, overwhelmed by the events of the previous night. Monica and Marion had retired to their bedroom after the long and difficult conversation.

When they both went downstairs for breakfast, they found Juan Manuel and Valeria still awake. They were worried about their reactions to the previous night's conversation and felt remorse to have been the cause of their sorrow.

Marion greeted them both and said," Discovering my past, although painful, in no way changes my feelings about my dear parents or my dear sister Mayina. I'm pleased to learn that I was born out of love and happiness, that life blessed me with an honorable family that loved me very much. My parents have my eternal gratitude and respect; they earned it. Both of you have regained what you long pined for; the doors of a happy future are now open to you. I truly am sorry for all that you suffered, what you, Valeria spend every day thinking about and suffering the loss of your daughter. But for me, a document or a confession means nothing. With Monica, the ties that unite us began well before knowing of our common parentage. I ask you to understand me. My difficulty will now be Mayina and how she will react to the news. As for the rest, time will tell."

With this she embraced them all, thanking Juan Manuel for the hospitality and making it known she was ready to return to Caceres.

After the car was packed and ready to leave, Monica reminded her father of the public report that Chief Caruso would be giving. Looking at Marion, he said, "Dear, we'll have to reserve lodgings at your hotel, do you think we can do that?"

"With pleasure, we'll expect you in a couple of days," she replied, drying tears that welled up in her eyes.

<><> CHAPTER FORTY-ONE <><>

After the funeral service, Mayina and Mariano were making their way, hand in hand, toward the restaurant when Mayina said," Only three people have shared my dreams, hopes and sorrows, Teresa, Dario and Marion. Our friendships have enabled us to know ourselves, how we are and how we think. You have given me support in these times of trouble---support that I desperately needed."

When they reached the hotel, they went straight to Mayina's room where she pulled out, from amongst her clothing, the little music box.

She took out the letter and, handing it to him, said, "You have to promise me that you will keep this secret until God dictates otherwise."

They left the room and sat in the living room underneath a light where Mariano read the document.

A few minutes passed in silence. Then, folding the papers, he said, "Here's my response to what my father said years ago…this person, so beloved…is Marion, his daughter, my sister!"

She responded, "So, now, Mariano you know why I've been so upset!

Taking her in his arms, he said, "My silly little beloved, knowing how Marion is, do you really believe that this would matter to her? The tenderness and closeness between both of you, nothing could destroy it! What really matters is what you feel, what lives in your heart, Mayina. Don't torture yourself, my angel. You'll see that everything will work out. You should follow the advice of those who love you. Don't let the past damage your present! We mustn't judge those who sin, just accept the reality."

Today life has given me something wonderful…a sister! You see how life can give us something new and fascinating each day?"

Kissing her very softly on the cheek, he whispered, "Thank you so much for confiding in me. Let's go back to the hotel."

<>< > CHAPTER FORTY-TWO <><>

The farewells had depressed them into silence as they drove on the highway towards the mountains. Behind them lay the city, with its different way of life, the urban noises, the port and its people. They were returning to the town where everything was different. Monica was looking forward to her new life with her fiancé, and Marion to her sister and the restaurant. The days spent at the Avolea home had made their mark on her heart, giving rise to feelings she'd never had before and to which she never wanted to return.

Her life was in Caceres; she had grown up here and expected to die there, in her beloved village.

In Caceres there were no lies, secrets or plots twists. In her mind was only on thing, her sister, the only thing that filled her with peace and happiness.

From the mountains the view was wonderful; the heat and humidity gave rise to the clouds that covered the valley, leaving visible only the highest summits.

In the distance one could see the road zigzagging, disappearing in spots amidst the clouds and giving them the illusion of gliding into is slopes.

Monica was the first to break the silence, asking, "What do you think about all that's happened, Marion?"

"It grieves me to have been the cause of so much sadness and suffering. I think that, for fear of losing me, my parents stayed quiet about the truth."

"I admire you your noble heart, your generous spirit and your ability to forgive, Marion. It makes me proud to be part of your life. I want to ask you something, something very important to me, "Would you like to be the maid of honor at my wedding?"

"I'd be proud to be; Marion answered, I accept with great pleasure!

They arrived late in the day at the village, as everyone was attending the funeral mass.

Sara and Carmela were glad to see them. They decided to unpack and wait for the mass to finish and surprise the group with the early return.

They were at the hotel's entrance when they heard the voices of others returning. When Dario and Teresa entered, the both rushed forward to greet them; Monica hugged her fiancé and kept saying how much she had missed him. Later Mayina and Mariano arrived, joining the welcome. Marion, in tears, hugged her sister, saying, "You don't know how much I missed you, Mayina. A few days seemed like centuries. "I have so much to tell you…!"

"Me, too, Marion. I am happy to see you back home!", Mayina responded.

It was nearly midnight when, drained by their trip, they finally went to bed.

<><> CHAPTER FORTY-THREE <><>

The entire population of the town congregated that morning at the church. Everyone wanted to say their final farewell to Father Jacob. After the service was over, his remains were carried to the local cemetery where they were buried for eternal repose.

Afterwards, nearly everyone returned to their regular Sunday routine, leaving a group to help in the chapel.

Dario and Monica decided to take advantage of the beautiful weather and ride horses on the outskirts of the town. Marion and Mayina got together in the office to discuss what had happened during the previous days.

"Tell me, Marion, how was it in the city?" she asked with some concern.

Putting aside her papers, she answered, "The trip was very nice. I got to see the outskirt of the city and Avolea's large home; I enjoyed going shopping with Monica. Mostly, it was very pleasant. But tell me, how are things with you? I was very disturbed to see you so upset. Are you better now?"

"I've been feeling better since I spoke with Mariano Mayina, said. He put my mind at rest a little. I promise I'll tell you later. But also, you know, he purchased the home that we went to see in the Forest Zone and it made me so sad."

"Why does that make you sad, or is there something else?", Marion asked.

"Marion, I've fallen crazily in love with him, didn't you notice? If he leaves I'll never see him again!"

"My little daydreamer. Finally your prince has arrived. I'm so happy for you."

"But you don't understand, Marion. He doesn't know", she answered between sobs.

"Let time teach him what has grown inside you, for now calm yourself and tell me what you have to say."

"I'm sorry, Marion, I don't think I can right now."

"Well then, I'll tell you what I learned while I was at Juan Manuel's house."

Sitting down next to her and taking her hands in hers, she looked at her very seriously and, with tears in her eyes, said to her, "But first I want to tell you that, out of love for ours parent's memory, my feelings have not changed, you understand? Nothing and no one will ever change what you mean to me."

"Marion, I don't understand, what are you trying to say?"

"Let me finish…. It's very difficult, but it's true."

<><> CHAPTER FORTY-FOUR <><>

After Marion had finished recounting the tale of her birth to her sister, they embraced and cried together, knowing that love bound them together more than dry facts. It was no matter that piece of paper stated otherwise; their souls would continue as one thanks to the caring and even-handedness they received from their parents.

Once they recomposed themselves, they left the office, full of peace, and joined the others in the dining room. Marion, Dario, Teresa and Monica and the priests were waiting for them and invited them to sit at their table.

Mariano seemed nervous and worried. Mayina asked, "Has something happened? You seem strange."

"This is the first time I am doing this", he said rising from his seat, and kneeling down next to her.

"Mariano, what's going on? Are you feeling sick? what's the matter?"

"I'm ill, very ill and my only salvation is you", he said, taking out a small jewelry case. His eyes full of love, he took her hand and said, "In the eyes of God and my family, I'm asking you to be my wife, my beloved."

Amazed Mayina extended her ring finger and answered, "Before God and all here present, I accept you offer to be my husband, my love."

Sealing the mutual promise before all gathered there with them, they kissed each other and everyone responded with applause and congratulatory words.

At the same time, handing some papers to Mayina, he said, "All princess need a castle; even though for now it's small, with time and our love its domains will grow."

With surprise and pleasure, she understood that they were the titles to the property on the hill, in both of their name.

"Mariano, so many lovely surprises! I thought you weren't aware of my feelings."

"For the first day I saw you, I knew that life would bind us forever. I love you, Mayina, with all my heart, as one can love only once in a lifetime. You make me a very happy man by accepting."

"Thank you, my love, for making me so fortunate."

<><> CHAPTER FORTY-FIVE <><>

They enjoyed their diner amidst the joy of the moment and plans for the future. Only those in the dining room remained when Juan Manuel, Valeria and Alejandro Zucareno arrived. They had all made the trip to attend the final public conference on the attack on Mariano and Don Javier.

Once everyone had been introduced, Alejandro approached Marion; looking at him with suspicion said, "Forgive me my audacity, but I don't think you know how to treat people…that is, women; in this town we treat each other with respect and dignity."

To which he responded, "Miss Mangual, I apologize for my uncouth behavior. Please forgive me."

Sealing the beginning of a new friendship, he elegantly kissed her hand.

Before retiring for the night, Juan Manuel asked Monica and Mariano to come to his room, as they had something important to discuss.

As they were walking towards their father's room they both wondered what could be so important that it couldn't wait.

They knocked on the door and he let them in.

Nervously, he asked them not to interrupt him, he began saying," My children, in the last few days much has happened, bringing us both sorrow and pleasure. I don't know if Monica has told you what happened at our house. With Marion's arrival there still remains something I must clarify to you, Mariano. It's time for you to know this. I want to be the one who tells you, since tomorrow you will have the proof of what I'm about to say."

"When I met your mother, she brought to our marriage a child under a year old. Life had treated her badly, leaving her alone with two little boys, identical twins. She would have to separate them. I don't know how, but she had to escape her situation, taking only one of them with her…you, Mariano; the other one she never went back for, until many years later."

"My error was in not telling you the truth in order to avoid hurting you or your mother. We raised you as our own child, although your mother never stopped living with sorrow and fear that your brother was walking down the wrong road in life. He took advantage of our position, extorting money for this silence about your mother's past. I also kept silent to protect your mother. Believe me, it wasn't easy to keep him at bay."

"He is a bad man, with no scruples, who resents that it was you and not he who enjoyed growing up in the bosom of a family, and more. I ask your forgiveness that I can finally tell you the truth. As a father, I gave you all my love, as if you had been my own. Please forgive me."

Without missing a beat, Mariano embraced his father and said, "It's not my place to forgive or judge you, I can only thank you for giving me your name and a home. Now I understand our poor mother, how much she must have suffered. I hope that God keeps her in peace; she will always have my gratitude and my love.

Monica had listened to her father recount the story. The only thing that mattered to her was to accept what our destiny brings us, leaving the past in oblivion.

She kissed her father and her brother and left to rest, as she had no further interest in the matter.

<<<>>>

<><> CHAPTER FORTY-SIX <><>

Chief Caruso was ready to begin the conference. He arrived in the company of Officer Puerta and the policeman Aronca. As so many were interested in the results of the investigation, a lot of people had turned out for the affair. Addressing the group, he said, "As a public servant, I want to be sure that you know, in a concise and accurate account, what we have compiled."

The attack on Misters Javier Molina and Mariano Avolea was carried out by a band of miscreants and directed by their leader, the culprit Leandro Quesada. The latter was motivated by personal revenge and arrived in our town with the express purpose of tracking the daily movements of the injured party. As you know, we were able to apprehend them thanks to information we received from the public and to the perseverance of the authorities."

"As soon as this meting concludes, they will be transferred to the city for judgment and sentencing. Lastly, I must remind you that it is the duty of all or you to continue to protect and maintain the peaceful and pleasant way of life in our valley."

He then approached Mariano and the family members to follow him to his office. He had something personal that he wanted to discuss with them.

Following the lead of the police Chief, Mariano and all the family proceeded towards the office.

Seated there next to two guards was Leandro Quesada who, at the sight of them, began to swear furiously.

Once he was brought under control and looking straight at his twin brother, he shouted, "I hate you, I've hated you all my life, and I won't rest until I see you dead! You were given everything in life, while I had to go begging to survive!!"

In silence the group watched the most unlikely scene of their lives; there together, the two identical brothers, which destiny had separated as children, looked into each other's faces for the first time…

Most sincere gratitude and Thank you to: Maria de los Angeles Roccato, (Angeles) for her dedication, effort and knowledge in the Composure of this book, to Carolyn Coble for the translation to English and to my husband Richard for his support.

SOME day, I will return to the village of Caceres, to the Marion and Mayina Mangual story and to the people that live in that beautiful valley at the foot of the mountains.

It will be a pleasure to find how their lives have evolved with the passing of time and how the pioneers with their faith and their love had worked to maintain the peace, tranquility and the simple of life with the arrival of tourists, strangers and the new settlers.